HOT DOG! 3

CIRCUS TIME!

FOR KY AND ISLA.—A.D

TO MY CAT, CATALIE PORTMAN . . .
OH, AND MY WIFE, CLARE.—D.M

Text copyright © 2017 by Anh Do
Illustrations by Dan McGuiness

All rights reserved. Published by Scholastic Inc., *Publishers since 1920.* SCHOLASTIC and associated logos are trademarks and/or registered trademarks of Scholastic Inc.

The publisher does not have any control over and does not assume any responsibility for author or third-party websites or their content.

This book is a work of fiction. Names, characters, places, and incidents are either the product of the author's imagination or are used fictitiously, and any resemblance to actual persons, living or dead, business establishments, events, or locales is entirely coincidental.

ISBN 978-1-338-58722-7

1 2020

Printed in the U.S.A. 23
This edition first printing 2020

Typeset in YWFT Mullino.

ANH DO

ILLUSTRATED BY
DAN McGUINESS

HOT DOG! 3

CIRCUS TIME!

Scholastic Inc.

ONE

My name's Hotdog. I'm like a regular dog, but **l-o-n-g-e-r!**

me!

This is my
friend **Kevin**.

Being a cat, Kev loves **napping**.
Sometimes he even falls asleep
when he's **eating lunch**.

MMM,
SLEEP-
EATING.

zzZZZ

FRIES

This is my friend **Lizzie**.

Lizzie **loves reading** funny stories.

Lizzie loves reading just as much as she **loves surprising people**.

Sometimes she does both **at the same time**. That's easy to do when you're a lizard that can blend into **anything**.

Usually the three of us are **really happy** together. Somehow we always find a way to **have fun**, no matter what the day brings . . .

If it's rainy outside . . . we call it **SLIPPERY SLIDE DAY!**

WEEEEEEEEE!

Or if it's snowing . . . we call it time for a

SNOWBALL FUN FIGHT!

Or if we've gone to the beach and the water's **too cold** for swimming ...

F-F-F-F-FREEEEZING!

. . . we find **something else** to do
that's fun . . .

Like building **sand costumes!**

But today we were all **a bit sad** ...
and none of us could figure out a way
to make things **ANY** better.

We were sad because we were **saying
goodbye.**

Lizzie was **leaving.**

We'd been friends **forever.** Ever since
we first met beneath the old pine tree
at the park.

We'd been **best buddies** ever since!

But that was until Lizzie decided to run away with the **circus!**

TWO

Lizzie was joining her sister, **Emma**, who was in the circus that was visiting town. Emma was a **trapeze artist.** She was famous for her high-flying **flips and tricks,** way up in the air.

Her trapeze partner, **Ribbit**, another amazing acrobat, was always there to **catch her**.

Together they were **un-frog-gettable!** They'd traveled through town after town, amazing the crowds with their daring **high-flying** skills.

But Lizzie didn't want to become a trapeze artist because Lizzie **HATED** **heights**. She even felt dizzy on stairs!

Lizzie wanted to join the circus to make people laugh! She wanted to be a **CLOWN!**

We'd helped her find some **pants** that were **too big**, a **funny bow**, and a **huge** pair of **shiny shoes**.

We made a red nose out of **a ball**, and a wig out of an **old mop**.

INTRODUCING . . .

Next, we had to help Lizzie practice her circus act.

First there was **juggling**.

Lizzie was already good ... but we quickly learned that you shouldn't practice juggling with **teacups**.

Then there was the **squirting flower.**

At first, we couldn't get it to point the right way. It kept **squirting Lizzie in the face!**

But when Lizzie saw us laughing at her, she decided to **leave it** that way!

Then there was **MIMING**. Miming is **pretending** to do something with actions and no words.

Loopy Lizzie was pretending she was **inside a glass box.**

She was **SO GOOD** at pretending she was trapped inside a glass box that Kev ran and got a hammer **to break her out!**

Lastly, Lizzie wanted to practice riding around in a **tiny** car.

We bought a secondhand car from a **mouse family** down the street.

IT'S PERFECT!

My friend was all packed and ready
to leave . . .

I wasn't ready to **say goodbye** yet.
I didn't know whether I ever would be!

"Lizzie," I said. "How about Kev and I walk you to the **big top tent**? We can help you with your bags. And then we can say goodbye . . . properly."

"Thanks, Hotdog," said Lizzie, looking up at me **with sad eyes**. "That'd be great."

Lizzie was one **tough lizard**, but I
was pretty sure she was going to miss us.

A lot.

HONK!
HONK!

THREE

I t was so hard saying **goodbye** to Lizzie.

THANKS FOR EVERYTHING, YOU GUYS.

BYE, LIZZIE. YOU'LL BE GREAT. GOOD LUCK!

Kev and I stood there watching our friend walk away, until she **disappeared** inside the big top tent.

"I wish we could **watch** the show tonight," said Kev. "It'd be **great** to see Lizzie in her very first show."

"You're right," I said. "We should **buy tickets!**"

But when we ran to the ticket booth, we couldn't believe the price! It was **$50** a ticket! We'd need **$100** for both of us to get into the show!

We'd said goodbye to our friend Lizzie, and now we couldn't afford tickets to see her being a **clown.**

Luckily, I remembered that we **never give up!**

"There's always a way!" I said.

Somehow, we would **raise the money** for the tickets, in time for the show.

Just then a truck drove by with an ad for **dog shampoo** on the side.

And that's when I got a **great** idea...

A dog wash!

We'd found an old plastic **wading pool**, some **soap**, and **sponges**. We were ready to go!

We only needed to wash **ten** dogs and we'd have all the **money** we needed!

DOG WASH! TEN DOLLARS! COME GET YOUR DOG WASHED!

DOG WASH $10

Kev was **dancing around** and calling out to everyone who passed by. I'd never seen Kev so excited! It was clear he **REALLY** didn't want to miss seeing Lizzie at the circus!

And neither did I!

DOG WASH!
JUST TEN DOLLARS!
WE PROMISE NOT
TO BE RUFF!

Hours passed, and it seemed **no dogs** wanted to be washed.

Just when we were about to pack it all up . . . we had our **first** customer.

He was a tiny brown Chihuahua called
Snowflake.

"Snowflake?" Kev whispered in my ear.
"I wonder why he's called that . . ."

"Let's not worry about that," I whispered
back. "Let's just **get washing**."

Snowflake was so small, we almost **lost him in the bubbles.**

And once we were done, Kev only had to blow on him once to dry him.

And then we understood why he was called **Snowflake!**

He looked **completely different**
when he was clean! He was actually white!

Because Snowflake was so small, it was
only fair we charged him **half price**.

"That'll be five dollars," I said.

At this rate we'd **never make enough** money in time for the show.

We needed a **better** plan.

We needed **MORE** animals.

We needed **BIGGER** animals.

We needed . . .

TO SET UP NEXT TO THE CIRCUS!

FOUR

"**T**his spot looks perfect," I said to Kev, as we **pulled up** next to the big top.

We were in between the big top entrance and the circus camp.

I lifted my nose in the air. **"Sniff, sniff."**

EW.

It smelled like there was an elephant or two that really needed **a good bath!**

"Smells like **two tickets** to the show!" said Kev.

Right away, **a crowd** gathered around us. Everyone wanted to **look their best!**

It was lucky we had **a LOT** of **soap!**

Two **grimy monkeys** jumped in the water first.

Ginger was up next.

He was a **Lion** with **VERY BIG TEETH** and **VERY BIG CLAWS.**

He also had an **amazing** mane. It took us forever to wash it!

Afterward, Ginger looked beautiful!

Next up was a **giraffe** called **Neck**.

"How on earth are we going to get up there?" Kev asked.

"Anyone got **a ladder**?" I asked the crowd.

"Who needs a ladder when you have us?" said the monkeys. They **clicked their fingers** and a whole **bunch** of monkeys appeared behind them.

In seconds,
the monkeys
had built a
ladder for us
to climb!

55

We washed two piggy-backing **pigs**, a three-humped **camel** called Humphrey, a muddy **hippo**, a very fancy **flamingo** ...

. . . and lastly, **Jellybean.**

The elephant!

SPLASH!

That was the **LONGEST WASH EVER.**

But finally we had **enough money** for tickets to the show! We did it!

FIVE

Kev and I **ran** for the big top!

The seats were already starting to fill up for the **big show** with **loads of excited kids** and families.

"Mmm, smells like **popcorn**," said Kev, drooling. **"My favorite."**

"We can have some later," I said to Kev. "But right now, we have to **find Lizzie**. We should let her know we're here to **cheer her on!**"

A **helpful duck** pointed to Lizzie's dressing room. That would be where she was getting ready.

"Hotdog! Kev!" Lizzie cried out. "What are you doing here?"

"We're here to see the show!" I said.

"But hey, what happened to your **clown outfit?**" said Kev. "Did it **shrink?**"

OH, THIS? WELL . . .

At that moment, a **fancy frog** and a lizard that looked a bit like Lizzie walked in together.

It was the **incredible Emma and Ribbit!** But they didn't look very happy. Or incredible. In fact, Emma had her arm **in a sling**.

"Lizzie's filling in for me," said Emma. "She's the **only one** at the circus who could fit into my costume."

She looked **nervous**. *Really* **nervous**.

"Lizzie," I said, "are you sure you're going to be **okay** up there?"

Lizzie gulped. "I'll be okay," she said unsurely. "I'll have **Ribbit** up there with me . . ."

AND I REALLY NEED TO HELP MY SISTER . . .

"Well, you **ARE the bravest** lizard we know," said Kev.

I nodded. "That's for sure. You are an amazing lizard who can do **ANYTHING**."

"Anything?" said Lizzie.

"Anything!" we agreed.

EVEN THE
DEATH-DEFYING
BACKWARD
TRIPLE
SPIN-FLIP?

"The **WHAAAAAT?**" I said.

"Zee **Death-Defying Backward Triple Spin-Flip**," said Ribbit in a smooth, swampy voice.

"Zee lovely lady **swings down backward** on zee bar, hanging by her toes. Zen she **flips and spins** high into zee air, three whole times!"

Ribbit held his hands up high above him. "And zen I catch her. **Easies!**"

Lizzie looked **so scared**. How was she going to pull this off?

The sound of **drumming** filled the big top.

BOM-BOM BO-BOM-BOM!

"It's **showtime!**" said Ribbit excitedly.

"I guess we'd better go find our seats,"
I said to Kev.

I **really hoped** our friend would be okay.

GOOD LUCK, LIZZIE.

SIX

It turned out the very fancy flamingo was actually the circus **ringmaster!** The monkeys and the piggy-backing pigs performed **awesome moves** while galloping around the arena.

Neck, the giraffe, was what you call a **contortionist**.

That's a big word that means you're **REALLY BENDY.**

OUCH!

The **lion tamer** was actually
Ginger, the lion! He'd tamed a pack of
wild poodles and trained them to
launch off a seesaw and leap through
rings of fire!

"You guys are **on fire!**" Kev yelled out, and the crowd cheered **wildly**. "No, seriously, one of you is on fire!"

Luckily, Jellybean the elephant was nearby with a trunk **full of water**.

Next up was the **Unbelievable Hippo Cannonball!**

The muddy hippo we'd given a bath earlier was **squeaky-clean** and **squished** into a cannon!

It was a **tight** squeeze!

The helpful duck lit the cannon and stood back, **covering his ears.**

We all waited for **AGES** ... but nothing happened. It looked like the hippo was **stuck!**

The duck **quacked** and ran around the front of the cannon to try and help **loosen him**. He was wedging a walking stick around the edges, when suddenly—

KABOO

The pair of them **went flying** and
ripped right through the big top roof!

The powerful cannon must have blasted them farther than ever before!

ARGGGH!

There was a **huge splash** in the
distance. The hippo and duck had landed
in a **muddy pond** nearby.

THAT WAS EGG
ZILARATING!

THIS IS MY
LUCKY DAY!

Once the crowd settled down again, the ringmaster stepped into **the spotlight**.

NOW INTRODUCING . . . THE ASTONISHING, HIGH-FLYING LOOPY LIZZIE AND RIBBIT!

It was time!

Lizzie was on!

The spotlight moved to the trapeze pair. Lizzie's face was looking **pretty woozy . . .**

Was she **ready** for this?

"Come on, Lizzie," Kev and I called out. **"You can do it!"**

Lizzie **wibbled and wobbled** her way up the ladder. Her whole body looked like jelly!

Meanwhile, Ribbit **leapt up** his side in just a few easy bounds.

Lizzie looked so small up at the very top. It was **so high!**

I CAN'T DO IT. I CAN'T DO IT. I CAN'T DO IT.

"Go, Lizzie!" we cheered again.

Slowly, she crawled to her feet and grabbed the trapeze bar.

She was trembling **SO MUCH** that she must have slipped.

Ribbit took that as his cue to swing out and catch her for their very first trapeze move.

He **jumped up and dove down,** swinging toward her.

"Let go!" I shouted out. **"Lizzie, let go!"**

I don't know whether she let go, or her toes slipped, but suddenly Lizzie was **soaring toward Ribbit**. This trick was happening whether she wanted it to **or not!**

Kev was so worried that he switched from eating his popcorn to **biting his nails.**

CHEW
CHEW
CHEW

It was **amazing**. Ribbit swung and caught Lizzie, they swung back together, then Lizzie was flung **into the air!** Somehow, she landed on her feet, back on her platform.

I couldn't believe she'd made it. Her **first trapeze trick!**

The crowd **cheered!**

Emma **jumped** joyfully below!

THAT'S MY SIS UP THERE!

Ribbit **kept on swinging**, moving from his hands . . . to his feet . . . to his nose . . .

At one point, he even **twirled up** into the air, caught the other trapeze bar with **his TONGUE**, swung around full circle, and landed perfectly once more, back on his platform.

This was all leading up to **THE BIG ONE**... The trick that would be toughest of all for Lizzie!

BEHOLD! THE DEATH-DEFYING BACKWARD TRIPLE SPIN-FLIP!

Kev could barely look. He tried to cover his eyes, but the only thing he had was **two donuts.**

103

Lizzie stood **bravely** on the edge of the platform. She hooked her toes over the trapeze bar.

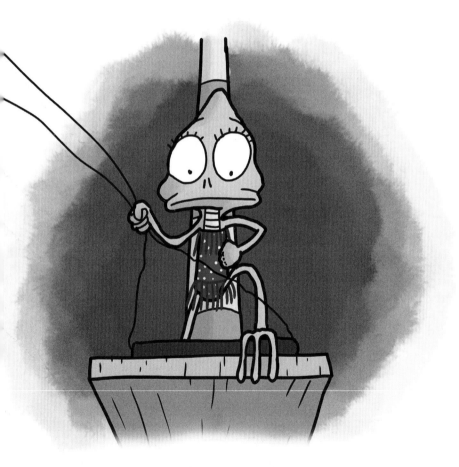

Now all she had to do was wait for
Ribbit's signal—**a soft croak**—
and jump off.

Kev and I held our breath!

Then came the **CROAK!**

Ribbit was off! Lizzie had to follow!

Lizzie swung down fast, backward, then began **flipping and spinning** up in the air.

One flip!

Two flips!

Three flips!

It was time for Ribbit to catch her . . .
but Lizzie **kept going!**

four flips! five flips!

She'd done FIVE FLIPS! That was **TOO many** flips!

The audience cheered **so loudly**, I had to cover my ears!

But now that Lizzie was finally on her way back down, Ribbit **wasn't going to be there** to catch her—he was already swinging back toward his platform.

They weren't going to make it!

There was no way Ribbit was going to catch her in time!

I grabbed Kev.

WE HAVE TO DO SOMETHING!

Kev and I **jumped out of our chairs** and ran outside.

We were running back through the door as **Lizzie fell!**

"RUN!" I shouted to Kev. **"QUICK!"**

We ran as fast as we could . . .

The crowd **gasped!**

We'd made it **just in time!**

Lizzie **leapt up** and held her hands in the air, proudly.

The crowd fell silent . . .

NAILED IT!

Lizzie jumped out of the wading pool,
took a deep breath, and **bowed!**

... And then suddenly everyone burst
into **huge cheers and laughter.**

The crowd went **absolutely WILD!**
They began chanting Lizzie's name.

SEVEN

"I had fun tonight," said Lizzie, "even though I nearly barfed **at least ten times** . . . *AND* I almost splattered on the ground **like an egg.**"

BUT YOU CAN HAVE THIS BACK.

"You were **amazing**," said Emma.

"Zee best!" added Ribbit. "Five whole spins! **You were magnificent!**"

Lizzie was pretty great on the trapeze. But she'd be even better **as a clown!**

The crowd **LOVED her** and thought she was so funny!

"Thanks, guys, but the trapeze is not for me," said Lizzie. "I'd much rather be **right here** with my feet on the ground . . ."

RIGHT HERE, WITH THESE TWO.

I looked at Lizzie. Right here? **With us?**

Did that mean she was staying?

"That was **kind of fun**, but I just want to be here with **my best friends**."

AW, I LOVE YOU GUYS!

Ever since she flew on the trapeze, Lizzie's been feeling **much braver** with heights. She even slept on her **top bunk!**

← very high!

And maybe, **when the circus comes around again . . .**

. . . we can **all run off together!**

MORE ADVENTURES COMING SOON!